Book Club Edition

**WALT DISNEY PRODUCTIONS**

presents

# Robin Hood
## spins gold

**Random House** 🏠 **New York**

First American Edition

Copyright © 1979 by The Walt Disney Company. All rights reserved under International and
Pan-American Copyright Conventions. Published in the United States by Random House, Inc.,
New York, and simultaneously in Canada by Random House of Canada Limited, Toronto.
Originally published in Denmark as ROBIN HOOD SPINDER GULD by Gutenberghus Bladene,
Copenhagen. Copyright © 1978 by Walt Disney Productions.
ISBN: 0-394-84160-3     ISBN: 0-394-94160-8 (lib. bdg.)

Manufactured in the United States of America     7890  CDEFGHIJK

Prince John was an evil prince.
Prince John was a greedy prince.
He loved himself.
He loved his gold.
But he did not love the people
in his kingdom.

One day Prince John said to the Sheriff of Nottingham, "I have not collected money from the people in three weeks. It is time for a new tax."

"More gold should make you very happy, Sire," said his servant, Sir Hiss.

"And very rich," said the prince.

That very day, the Sheriff of Nottingham
posted a sign.
It said:

**NOTICE**

*Tomorrow morning
all the people of
Nottingham must
pay a tax of
100 gold pieces.*

The people were so worried.
How could they pay the tax?
No one had any gold.
Prince John had taken it all.

Luckily the poor people had a friend named Robin Hood.

He was an outlaw who lived in the woods. Friar Tuck and Little John lived with him. They were outlaws, too.

Robin Hood and his men did not like the greedy prince.

And the prince did not like them, either.

More than once they had stolen
Prince John's gold.

They gave it to the poor people.

So Prince John and the sheriff were always
looking for Robin Hood and his men.

When Robin Hood and Little John
went to town, they wore disguises.

That way they could find out
what was happening without being discovered.
They had many different outfits
to wear.

On the day of the new tax Robin Hood
dressed up as an old blind beggar.
And Little John dressed up as a woman.

They came to Prince John's sign.
A group of poor people were reading it.
They looked very sad.

"We will have to get Robin Hood's help,"
said an old woman.

"You will, indeed," said Robin.

He took off his dark glasses.

"Look!" said the people. "It is Robin Hood!"

"I have a plan
to help you,"
said Robin.

Just then the Sheriff of Nottingham came by.
Robin put his glasses back on fast!

"What is going on here?" asked the sheriff.

Robin answered, "I was telling these people
what I have heard. Robin Hood plans to rob
Prince John again."

"The prince would love to hear about this," said the sheriff. "Come with me."

So off they went.

The sheriff and Robin arrived at Prince John's castle.

"Who is this dirty beggar?" cried the prince.
"Get him out of here."

"But Sire," said the sheriff.
"This man has news of Robin Hood."

The prince's ears perked up.

"Tell me," said the prince.

"I heard Robin Hood talking," said Robin.

"He plans to steal your gold tonight."

"I will double the guard!" cried Prince John.
"No, no!" said the sheriff. "Triple the guard!"

"Sire," hissed Sir Hiss,
"it does not matter
how many guards you have.
Robin Hood will trick you anyway."
    "Quiet, Hiss!" yelled Prince John.

"I know how you can trick Robin Hood,"
said beggar Robin.

"You DO?" cried the prince.

"Yes," said Robin. "I have a daughter
who can spin straw into gold."

"So?" asked Prince John.

"So I will bring my daughter here,"
said Robin. She will spin all your gold
into straw. When Robin Hood gets here,
he will find straw—not gold! He will not
steal straw!"

Prince John
scratched his head.
"But how
do I get
my gold back?"

"That's easy," said Robin. "My daughter
will leave her magic spinning wheel here.
Then you can spin the straw back into gold
yourself."

"Oh, goody!"
cried Prince John.
"At last
I will trick
Robin Hood!"

Robin Hood said he would be coming at midnight," added Robin. "So I will leave now to get my daughter. We should be back in plenty of time."

Sir Hiss thought
the idea
was a trick.

"Sire," he hissed, "This is..."
"Stop hissing in my ear!" roared Prince John.

He turned to Robin Hood.
"Farewell, my good man," he said.

Robin Hood quickly
left the castle.

He went back to the woods
where Little John was waiting.
"Put on your disguise again," said Robin,
"and come with me. I will tell you why
on the way to the castle."

Robin Hood and Little John
arrived at the castle.
Little John was carrying
a spinning wheel.

The guard took
Robin and Little John
to the prince.

"So you will spin
my gold into straw,"
Prince John said
to Little John.

"Come with me. Hurry!"
Robin Hood and Little John
followed Prince John.

The Royal Counting House was surrounded by guards.
Prince John walked past them.
So did Robin Hood and Little John.

They went inside.
The counting house
was full of gold.
Bags of it were piled
high to the ceiling.

"Spin away, my dear," said Prince John.

Little John set up his spinning wheel.
But he did nothing else.
"My daughter is shy," said Robin Hood.
"She cannot spin if you are watching."

"Very well," said Prince John.
"Just knock on the door
when you are finished.
The guards will show you out."

Little John and Robin Hood got busy
at once. They tied the bags of gold
to a rope. They dropped the rope
out the window.

Friar Tuck was waiting below in a boat.
He emptied out the gold.
Then he stuffed the bags with straw.
Robin pulled the rope back up again.
Soon all the gold was gone.
The room was full of straw.

Friar Tuck's boat was full of gold.
He covered the gold with straw.

When all the gold was covered with straw,
he quickly rowed away.

Then Robin Hood
knocked on the door.
The guards opened it.
Prince John was waiting
outside.
He rushed in.

"I could not wait!" he cried.
Prince John looked at the straw.
"You have really done it!" he said.
"What a joke on Robin Hood!"
He clicked his heels in the air.

Then Prince John said, "You can go home now, old man.
Just leave your magic spinning wheel here.
I would pay you for it.
But I have no gold right now."

With that, Prince John went to his room.
He would wait there for the robber to come.

Robin and Little John went back to the woods.
Friar Tuck was waiting for them—with the gold.

Robin Hood and Little John gave bags of gold
to the poor people.
There was joy in Nottingham that night.

Meanwhile, Prince John was walking up and down.
Sir Hiss and the sheriff sat by a window.
They were waiting for Robin Hood to come.
It was past midnight.

"You have been tricked, Sire," hissed Hiss.

"Quiet, Hiss," said Prince John.
"You always worry too much."

"But the sun is up,"
hissed Hiss.
"And Robin Hood
is not here."

"Come with me," said the prince.
"I will show you
that this is no trick.
It does not matter
that Robin Hood
did not come."

Prince John took Sir Hiss and the sheriff
to the Royal Counting House.

"See," said the prince. "They spun the gold
into straw, just as they said they would."

"Sire!" yelled Hiss. "You have been fooled!"

"This is a disaster!" cried the Sheriff of Nottingham.

"No, no," said Prince John, smiling.
"Watch this."

The prince sat down at the spinning wheel.
He started to spin the straw.
But no gold came out.

"I know this will work,"
said the prince.

"It has to work!"

"Where is my gold!" he shouted.

But there was no gold, because Robin Hood
had tricked him again.